Title: Saving My Mate
Subtitle: Werewolf Shifter MF Romance Short Story
Author: Stacey Cannon

Copyright Page

From the Publisher:
Thank you for purchasing this book.

Table of Contents

Saving My Mate
Description

Tristan, an alpha, attacks and tries to subdue the rogue wolves without having any harm come to the human woman, Rhea. It is a struggle when the scent of her blood assails his nostrils and all logical thoughts flee his mind. His wolf howls in rage and ecstasy as one thought dominates his mind. A human woman is being captured and needs saving. The Alpha can't believe he has finally found his mate. In the blink of an eye, Tristan transforms into a huge coal-black wolf, his shredded clothes being the only indication that a man had stood there at all. He races forward as he watches the rogue wolf hit his mate and snarls in fury. Rhea knew who Tristan is. It takes time for her to accept the fact that she is Tristan's mate even though she finds him attractive from the first experience with him.

Chapter 1

Tristan Forest fisted his hand menacingly and snarled at the image before him. A beautiful young woman was being held tight against the body of one of the rogues while the other ran his hands down her neck and over her collarbone. The rogue's lethal claw grazed her delicate skin and the scent of her blood filled the night air, followed closely by the acrid scent of her fear. The girl struggled wildly and kicked out at the beast in front of her, landing a solid blow to his genitals. Her captor howled in fury and lashed out instantly, backhanding her face with such force that she was stunned by the blow and hung her head forward limply.

Tristan had been contemplating how best to subdue the rogue wolves without having any harm come to the human woman when the scent of her blood assailed his nostrils and all logical thought fled his mind. His wolf howled in rage and ecstasy as one thought dominated his mind. MINE!! The Alpha couldn't believe he had finally found his mate. In the blink of an eye, Tristan transformed into a huge coal-black wolf, his shredded clothes being the only indication that a man had stood there at all. He raced forward as he watched the rogue hit his mate and snarled in fury.

The rogues looked up startled at the black blur racing toward them and dropped the girl quickly, taking off toward the woods. Tristan howled again as he was torn between chasing after them and checking on his mate. His protective instincts won out and he ran to her, transforming into his human form mid-stride.

Rhea Blake swore under her breath as she shook her head to dispel the dizziness that had engulfed her for a moment after the man/animal thing had hit her. She watched in fascination as the huge black wolf morphed into a man just a few feet away from her and sucked in a breath at the gorgeous image that met her eyes. He was the most stunning thing she had ever laid her eyes on. Tall and firmly muscled with short dark hair and piercing emerald green eyes, the mystery man looked at her in concern before crouching down beside her. Rhea blushed as she realized he was stark naked and focused on his face to stop her eyes from drifting downward to what she was sure would be an impressive sight.

"Are you all right Little One?" he asked worriedly, fighting his instinct to gather her up in his arms and carry her off to claim her primitively.

"Uhm, yes, I'm fine, thank you," she responded cautiously.

"You were hit pretty hard. Can you stand up?"

"Yes, I'm sure I can," she said while trying to get to her feet. Rhea swayed as the world spun and then gasped as she felt strong arms encircling her body, making her dizzy for a different reason entirely.

"It's all right, I've got you," the stranger said comfortingly. "I'm Tristan Forest. What's your name?" he enquired, while guiding her to her car. Tristan gazed into the beautiful hazel brown eyes of his mate and tenderly brushed aside a lock of her wavy chestnut colored hair.

"Rhea. Rhea Blake," she answered.

"You have a beautiful name, Rhea."

"T-thank you," she stuttered.

"Let me get you to a hospital Little One so that we can have you checked out, okay?"

"What? No, that won't be necessary," she said. "Look I'm really grateful you scared them off but I'm fine and I don't think it would be smart to go anywhere with a naked werewolf right now," she said bluntly.

Tristan stared at his mate in shock. She knew what he was? Why wasn't she freaking out? Rhea looked into his eyes and almost laughed at the comical confused expression that was apparent in his strong features.

"Don't look so surprised Mr. Forest. It would hardly take a rocket scientist to figure it out. The idiots who attacked me sprouted claws and fur out of nowhere and you transformed from a wolf to a man in front of my very eyes. That's pretty solid evidence of what you are."

Tristan continued to stare at her, dumbfounded by her easy acceptance of all she had seen. Then common sense took over and his usual confident self-assurance shone through.

"Okay, so you figured out what we are. That doesn't change the fact that you were hit pretty hard and you're still bleeding. I'm going to fetch some clothes and take you to the hospital. And please call me Tristan," he ordered.

"No. Thank you for your concern, Tristan but no. I can take care of myself. I just need to replace this tire and I'll be good to go," she said decisively.

Tristan frowned at his mate's stubbornness and realised that trying to convince her would get him nowhere. He had to be clever about this.

"At least let me sort that out for you then Rhea. I'll put on some clothes first if it will make you more comfortable," he teased with a cocky grin.

Rhea sighed and decided to just let him sort out the tire. He obviously wasn't going to just let her leave and she did feel a bit woozy still.

"All right Tristan. But where are you going to find clothes now? In your hidden den?" she asked somewhat sarcastically.

Tristan grinned in response. "No, my sweet, it's just beyond the trees. Give me a second."

Rhea watched as he ran off toward the greenery and disappeared into the dense foliage. She had a feeling that Tristan Forest was going to be trouble, in the most delicious of ways. She had to be wary with him or she knew she would be falling hard for him before she could even catch her breath.

Rhea watched as Tristan jogged back to her in just a pair of loose jeans. She was surprised that he had actually found a pair of jeans in the forest but she figured werewolves thought ahead about these things. He was much taller than she was, probably around 6'3 and he oozed strength and masculinity. Her eyes were drawn to his defined abs and pectoral muscles and she immediately felt the urge to run her hands and her tongue over every inch of his body. Rhea blushed at the direction her thoughts were traveling in. She was still a virgin at twenty-four years old and had never been interested in anything physical with a man before. Granted, Tristan was not just a man, but he was still a stranger who had suddenly awoken primal thoughts and urges within her and she didn't know what to make of it.

Tristan gazed at his mate as he jogged toward her and noticed that she was lost in thought. He took the opportunity to absorb every detail about her that he could. She was of average height for a woman, around 5'6 but not petite. She had long wavy brown hair that he itched to run his hands through and a curvy figure. Tristan had to fight the urge to groan aloud as she bit her bottom lip while she was thinking and he finally met her heated hazel eyes before she blinked and seemed to shake herself back to the present. He jealously wondered what she had been thinking about that caused her to get that sexy intense expression on her face and decided to get to the task of changing her tire before he started demanding that she divulge every thought that passed through her mind.

"Pop the trunk my sweet. I'll need to get the jack and the spare tire."

Rhea did as he asked and then watched as he quickly and efficiently replaced her blown out tire with the spare one. Within minutes the car was ready to move.

"Thank you, Tristan. I appreciate your help," she said sincerely.

"It was a pleasure Rhea. Now let's get you to the hospital."

"Tristan, for the tenth time, I'm fine. I really don't need the hospital. And I'll be there later on anyway. So I'll get looked at then, okay?" she said somewhat impatiently.

"Why will you be there later on? Are you all right?" he demanded.

"Yes, I'm fine. I work there. I'm a nurse, which is how I know I'm fine. Is there anything else you need to know?" she asked sarcastically. Rhea wondered why she was being so prickly with him and then realised that it was because she was so intrinsically drawn to this man that it scared her. Everything about him called to her and she hated the fact that she actually liked his demanding tone and the way he seemed to expect obedience.

The easiest way to deal with it was sarcasm and anger. She wasn't naive enough to imagine that this divine creature would actually be interested in her so it would be safer for her to just part ways with him now and keep her heart secure from any possible future pain.

Tristan grinned at her annoyed tone before replying, "Just one other thing. What time do you get off work?"

"Noon," Rhea answered distractedly.

"I'll see you then Little One."

Rhea cursed herself for being so preoccupied and actually telling him the correct time that her shift would end but then realized that he would not know which hospital she worked at anyway. Nonetheless, she wouldn't be encouraging him regardless of how quickly he set her pulse racing.

"Look, I appreciate your help Tristan but I don't think it would be a good idea for us to socialize. You seem like a great guy and everything but there would be no point to us becoming friends."

Rhea looked up into his twinkling eyes and her breath caught in her throat even as she dreaded his response.

"I don't just want to be friends with you Rhea," he said in a deep voice full of promise. "You will be mine whether you know it yet or not."

Ignoring the fact that her heart had literally just skipped a beat, Rhea narrowed her eyes and got into her car. "We'll see about that Mr. Forest. Have a good evening."

Chapter 2

Before Tristan could stop her, Rhea started the car and drove off. She kept her eyes on him for as long as possible before breathing a sigh of relief and trying to calm her erratic heartbeat. She had no idea what Tristan had meant by his possessive words and she had no intention of finding out. Even if he did, by some miracle, come to the right hospital, she would not allow herself to be drawn in by him. She would be a notch on Tristan's bedpost no matter how much he drew her in.

Having resolved to avoid Tristan at all costs, Rhea headed home to shower before starting her shift. She worked odd hours at the hospital, taking the shifts that everyone else tended to avoid. Rhea had nobody to spend her free time with and wasn't inclined to meet new people since she had learned from experience that the people closest to you had the ability to hurt you the most. So, she instead focused her time and energy on the children in the pediatric ward of the Forest Hospital and it was by far the most fulfilling aspect of her life. Children were still innocent and loving without having ulterior motives.

Rhea loved the simplicity in the way kids thought. It was so much easier dealing with them as opposed to the endless mindless games adults played.

Rhea arrived home a few minutes later and allowed her mind to wander as she stepped into the shower, ignoring the throbbing heat between her legs that had been caused by Tristan's intense unwavering stare and sculpted muscles. The man exuded a powerful sexuality that Rhea could not help but react to and she wished that she had enough time to relieve the ache he had caused. But she had to get to her shift on time. So she brutally squashed the urge to bring herself to orgasm and proceeded to wash her hair instead.

Rhea had been happy, or at least as close as she could get, until meeting Tristan Forest. She knew she wasn't frigid or jilted. She had chosen to live her life without getting close to people for a good reason. But now Rhea found herself questioning her choices and her lonely existence. Tristan had unknowingly caused her to become dissatisfied with the course her life was on. She wondered how one man could have such a profound effect on her after one simple encounter.

Frowning as she got dressed in her simple blue scrubs and tennis shoes, Rhea thought about how she had gotten to this point in her life. She had been a happy child for the first few years of her life. Then things just went downhill and had never picked back up. Rhea considered everything she had been through a learning experience and so she had no regrets. That didn't stop her from wishing things had been different. She shook herself out of her funk, determined to not allow herself to become even more depressed than usual and left for work.

Rhea hoped that the day would bring would bring no further surprises. As much as she would love to see Tristan again, she knew that it would only lead to further heartache and she didn't know how much more of that she could take. Groaning aloud at the fact that her thoughts had once again returned to Tristan, Rhea prayed silently that she could forget him and the electrifying effect he seemed to have on her mind and her body.

***Tristan watched as Rhea drove off and chuckled at the way she had politely tried to get him to back off. He could tell that his mate was a feisty one and that he would have to be persistent with her. There was no way he would forget she existed. It simply wasn't an option. Tristan shifted into his wolf form and followed Rhea's car from a distance. He ran along the periphery of the woods and easily kept track of her all theway to her little cottage. He was surprised by the fact that she lived so close to the woods. He knew that that particular cottage was hardly ever occupied due to people being afraid of the occasional wild animal heard in the forest.

Tristan growled at the thought that his mate had been so close to the pack's compound all this time and he had not once scented her. He was usually very level-headed but his wolf was impatient to mate with Rhea and he could find no compelling reason to hold the wolf at bay. His mate seemed to be fine with the idea of werewolves so all he needed to do was convince her that they were in fact soul mates and were destined to be together. It was that simple. Tristan groaned, knowing that this task was far easier said than done.

His thoughts were disturbed by the sound of running water and Tristan let out a strangled groan at the image of Rhea taking a shower. He could picture the water flowing smoothly over her naked smooth creamy skin and he shut his eyes in a futile attempt to escape the picture his mind had conjured up. Tristan waited a little while longer until he saw his mate exit the cottage and leave for work, his wolf only calm because he knew they would be seeing their mate later on that day.

Tristan sprinted back to the pack's compound to inform his betas that there would soon be an alpha female joining the ranks and to prepare for his meeting with Rhea. He was ecstatic and could hardly process the fact that he had actually found his life mate.

Tristan had waited for four hundred years and had been contemplating the idea that he just was not destined to find his mate. It was a ridiculous notion but he had watched many of his family and friends' mate with the one special person that fate had gifted them with while he remained alone. Now he had found his destiny and he knew that he had to tread carefully. Failure was not an option. Tristan linked telepathically to Aidan, his second in command, as he neared the compound.

Aidan, are you at the compound or at work?

I'm still at work Alpha. Am I needed at the compound? I'll leave immediately.

Oh cut the Alpha crap. We've been best friends for three centuries. I just have a question. Is there a Rhea Blake working at the hospital?

Yes there is. She's a nurse in pediatrics and she lives at that cottage on the south side of our border. Why do you ask Tris?

She's my mate Aid!! I've finally found her!! I can't believe she's been living near the compound and working at the hospital all this time and I never knew she was so close.

Well we know there's no such thing as coincidence brother. There must be a good reason why your meeting was delayed and I'm sure we'll find out soon enough. You know, this might not go down too well with the other females in the pack. They've been trying to get your attention for years and they won't take this too kindly. Not to mention the fact that she's human.

Yes I know there are some who won't be pleased but any disagreement will have to go through me. Besides, the mate that Luna gifted to me would not be meek and submissive. I know she'll be able to handle herself. I'm briefing the other betas in a few minutes. So I'll see what the reaction is like then.

Tristan closed off his mental link to Aidan as he shifted back into human form and entered his private living quarters. He took a quick shower and changed into a pair of black cargo pants and a plain black t-shirt before linking telepathically to his three other betas and calling a quick meeting in his study. The betas were in charge of various duties.

They were all fierce warriors but were also given great responsibility in helping Tristan rule the pack and the numerous corporations owned by them. Unlike most other wolf packs, Tristan had female betas as well as male and he trusted them all implicitly. He watched from the window as all three arrived at his cabin at the same time and smiled as Caden opened the door for the two women, Katrina and Alyssa. Tristan was unfailingly proud of the fact that all the men in his pack treated women with courtesy and respect, regardless of rank.

"Thank you all for heeding my call. This won't be long. I just have an announcement and then you all can return to whatever you were doing."

All three nodded and stood waiting for Tristan to continue.

"I have found my mate and will hopefully be bringing her to the compound soon. There may be issues with certain members of the pack since she is human. So I want you all to be aware and keep your ears open to any possible threat. I will not tolerate her being harmed by any other person, especially any pack members."

"T-man that's great news!! Wow!! I'm so happy for you!!" Caden congratulated Tristan. The tall sandy haired giant smiled cheekily while he clasped forearms with Tristan and thumped his back in the traditional way of greeting.

The two women expressed similar reactions and wished Tristan well in his pursuit of his mate. Tristan thanked them all and asked Caden to stay behind while he dismissed the two women.

"Cal I want you to be extra vigilant. I trust Kat and Alyssa but I know they might hesitate if their friends or family show dissent. I want you to be my right hand on this."

"Sure thing Alpha. Thank you for entrusting me with this. You know I won't let you down."

The two men shook hands before Caleb left Tristan's cabin. Tristan grabbed his car keys as soon as he was alone and headed off to the hospital, eager to see his mate once again.

***

Rhea found herself lost in thought more than once during her shift and mentally shook herself for her distraction. It had never happened to her before as she was always aware of her surroundings, especially at work. She cursed Tristan for invading her thoughts and focused on the files she was organizing. It was the worst part of her shift, the hour before she got off duty.

Rhea turned to grab the last file off the desk and gasped as she came face to face with Aidan Forest. The man was beautiful in a severe somber sort of way with short brown hair and piercing icy blue eyes. Rhea placed her hand on her throat in surprise at his sudden appearance. She was not at all used to being caught unaware and it was the second time in less than 24 hours that she had managed to get into an odd situation without even seeing any sign of it coming. The werewolves that had accosted her on the road had literally appeared out of nowhere and by the time Rhea realized that she was not alone they were too close for her to escape.

Rhea gazed at Aidan and briefly wondered at her complete lack of interest in him before she spoke. "I'm sorry Mr. Forest, I didn't realize you were there. Is there anything I can help you with?" she asked politely.

"No nurse Blake, not really. And please, call me Aidan. I've just come to inform you that another nurse has come in early so you may end your shift now, if you wish."

Rhea frowned as she wondered why the head surgeon would feel the need to inform her of shift changes but shrugged off the weird feeling before replying.

"It's just Rhea. And thank you for letting me know Aidan. I'll clock out now then. Have a good day."

"I'll walk you to the foyer Nurse Blake," Aidan said formally.

Rhea saw no way out of the situation without being rude and she really did not want to offend Aidan Forest of all people so she sighed in capitulation and walked to the staff changing room to collect her bag and change into her everyday sneakers. She emerged from the room half expecting Aidan to have disappeared but found him waiting in the exact position he had been in when she walked into the staff room. Rhea followed the imposing man to the elevator and wondered whether she should attempt to chat with him but dismissed the idea after glancing at his stony features. The man was the youngest and most successful heart surgeon in the country but he definitely needed to lighten up.

Rhea was so lost in thought that she was startled when the elevator bell chimed, signaling that it was at the hospital foyer. She turned to thank Aidan for escorting her but he had already turned away and was heading to the receptionist's desk. Rhea frowned at his odd behavior before slinging her bag diagonally across her shoulders and heading to the stairwell that led to the employees' parking facilities. She was suddenly shoved from the right and swore under her breath as she waited to feel the impact of hitting the porcelain tiles that decorated the foyer floor. After a few seconds Rhea forced her eyes open and gasped as her gaze was instantly snared by the half-irritated, half-amused emerald green eyes that had haunted her since last night. She groaned as he began speaking and she became aware of his strong arms wrapped around her.

"We've got to stop meeting like this my sweet," he grinned.

"Tell that to the idiot who decided I should become intimately acquainted with the floor. What are you doing here Tristan?"

"I told you I'd see you after your shift Rhea and I am a man of my word."

"You know, this could be considered stalking. What did you do, call every hospital in the city?"

"Nope, I just called Aidan," Tristan replied seriously.

Rhea glanced at him as if he was certifiable before the realisation of what he said actually sunk in.

"That snake!! That's why he randomly decided to escort me downstairs. He knew you'd be here!"

Tristan growled at the idea of Rhea being alone with an unmated male and his gaze turned feral as his wolf insisted, they mark their territory so every male would know that Rhea belonged to them.

"Okay really now, is the growling necessary?" she asked impatiently.

"Huh?" Tristan looked completely taken aback.

"What's with the growling under your breath? You're making the sick people uneasy."

Tristan looked around and realized that a few people were staring at him and Rhea.

"I don't like the idea of you being alone with any other male. Now you must be starving, I'm taking you to lunch Little One."

"What? Are you insane? Any other male? My God, why do I attract the loony ones? You show up at my work like a crazy stalker person and expect me to just come along with you? I don't think so Tristan. You must be out of your freaking—"

Rhea's tirade was suddenly cut off by the high-pitched squeak of her head nurse. Rhea winced at the sound before realizing that Nurse Stone was headed rapidly toward her and Tristan.

"Mr. Forest, oh what a pleasure to see you here, sir! We weren't expecting you today. Let me escort you to your office or is there anything else you would like me to help with?" she gushed.

Rhea frowned at the enthusiastic cnthrallcd tone coming from one of the scariest women on the planet. Tristan had to school his features so as to not laugh at his mate's obvious irritation.

"No thank you Nurse Stone. I'm just here to pick up my lunch date so that won't be necessary."

The large imposing woman's eyebrows shot up in surprise and she looked at Rhea for the first time since spotting Tristan. An expression of disbelief crossed her face before she turned back to Tristan.

"Lunch date? Well then let me know who the lucky lady is and I'll send Rhea here to fetch her for you."

"Actually, Rhea is my date Nurse Stone and I do believe I am the lucky one in the situation," Tristan said coolly. "That is if she would grace me with her presence," he teased Rhea.

Rhea was fuming at her supervisor's audacity and decided to play the situation up a bit. Nurse Stone always had it in for Rhea and now was her chance to exact her revenge. Ignoring the other woman's presence, Rhea saddled up to Tristan and looked him up and down as if considering what he had to offer.

"Oh, I'm not so sure Tristan. I mean I have quite a busy schedule today. I don't think there's enough time to fit you in," she said almost regretfully. Before Tristan could reply Nurse Stone cut in with an incensed gasp.

"Are you out of your mind?? Have some respect you insolent woman!! Don't you know who Mr Forest is!!??"

Chapter 3

Rhea tried not to laugh aloud at the irate shocked tone of Nurse Stone's voice as she chastised her for being so brazen. "I'm certain you'll be enlightening me on the topic..."

"You should be ashamed of yourself woman! How dare you be so disrespectful! I'll have you fired for your impertinence! Tristan Forest is the owner of Forest Industries and a great benefactor to this hospital. You should be honored that he even noticed you exist!" Nurse Stone almost shouted.

The thought that the head nurse might be perilously close to bursting a blood vessel crossed Rhea's mind before she replied, "If you must know, I am completely aware of who he is, Nurse Stone. And you can't fire me. You wouldn't know how to deal with the children otherwise. Now if you'll both excuse me, I have somewhere else I need to be."

With that said, Rhea turned and began walking once again to the stairwell. She became aware of a presence behind her and turned to face Tristan, not realizing how close behind her he actually was.

"Oomph!" she squeaked out as she almost collided with his strong frame. "Oh, dear Lord. For goodness sake, leave me alone you insufferable man," she said exasperatedly.

"Oh, no you don't. What do you mean you know exactly who I am? Why didn't you say anything? And why are you so hell bent on avoiding spending any time with me?" Tristan demanded.

" I don't have to explain anything to you," Rhea bit out tersely.

"Maybe not, but I'll get the answers out of you anyway," Tristan said with a decidedly predatory glint in his eyes.

"Try your worst Tristan, I'm not afraid of you," Rhea lied. She had no idea why she was being so evasive with him but her defenses were up big time and she always trusted her instincts. Although this time she wasn't certain exactly what she was afraid of. She just knew that the safest thing to do would be to run and not look back.

Tristan paused as he saw the lie in her eyes and heard her heart pounding harshly. His mate was afraid of him? He let go of her slowly and backed away, running a frustrated hand through his hair. Tristan had been tempering his usual dominant streak around Rhea but she was still afraid of him. The thought made his stomach clench and he wondered if he should give her more time and be less persistent. Perhaps she would be more amenable to spending time with him if he took things a lot slower. Tristan's train of thought was broken by a hesitant touch on his forearm and he looked into Rhea's confused, worried eyes.

"What's wrong?" she asked tentatively.

Rhea found herself becoming more and more concerned as Tristan had stood a few feet away from her running his hand through his hair. She knew that it would be the ideal time to walk to the parking lot quietly and just leave, but he looked almost defeated and the image did not sit well with her. Before she could stop herself, she realized that she had reached out to touch him. The spark she felt beneath her fingertips almost made Rhea gasp aloud, but she tempered her reaction and focused on his eyes instead.

Tristan took hold of Rhea's hand and placed a gentle kiss on her palm before replying. "Absolutely nothing, my sweet. I am truly sorry that I've caused you to become afraid of me. I haven't courted a human before and I suppose I'm doing it all wrong with you. I'll let you go home now if that's what you want."

Rhea read the sadness in his eyes and she felt her heart constrict at the thought that she had made him feel that way. Rhea was vaguely aware that she seemed to be in no control of her emotions at all but didn't question the sudden change of heart. She just knew with every fiber of her being that she could not ever hurt the gorgeous man in front of her. So she made a decision and hoped it would not backfire.

"You know, I could use a sandwich or something. Where are we going?" she asked.

"You don't have to come with me under duress, Rhea. I don't want you to feel obligated in any way, Little One," Tristan said although he was praying fervently that she did not take back her acceptance.

"I'm not under duress. I'm hungry. Now, lead on oh great benefactor," she teased.

Tristan chuckled before gallantly offering her his arm and they began walking out the hospital's front sliding doors. Rhea knew that her pulse was racing, although this time it was more in anticipation than fear. She hated how inconsistent she was being but decided she'd just go with her gut from now on.

"So are you going to tell me how you knew who I was?" Tristan asked casually.

Rhea grinned broadly before replying, "It would hardly take a rocket scientist to figure it out. Your name is legend and you had Aidan Forest, grouch extraordinaire, informed me that my shift was over. I just put two and two together."

Tristan led Rhea to a coal black '69 Camaro and unlocked the passenger door for her. "Oh wow! This is yours?" Rhea asked excitedly. "It's gorgeous!"

"Yep, she's mine. I restored her myself. I take it you like American muscle cars then, Little One?"

"It's a guilty pleasure. I've never owned one, but I love them. Show me what she can do Tristan. "

Tristan nearly groaned aloud at the excited husky timber of his mate's voice and clenched his fist as she let out a soft breathy moan when he started the engine and it hummed to life. Part of him was jealous of her reaction to the car and he grinned wryly at the thought that he was envious of an inanimate object.

Tristan drove fast but he was completely in control and Rhea loved every second. She was reluctant to leave the car when Tristan parked outside a little cafe and sighed regretfully before taking his hand and allowing him to help her step out of the amazing piece of machinery.

"You know, I should be hurt that you're already so in love with the car but won't even eat lunch with me without kicking up a fuss," Tristan sighed teasingly although there was an odd note in his voice.

Rhea blushed before mumbling, "I wouldn't be so hurt if I were you Tristan, you severely underestimate your appeal."

Tristan felt his wolf rumble its approval at the hint of their attraction being mutual and he felt himself cornering Rhea against the car without even thinking about what he was doing. Tristan placed his hands on the frame of the door and leaned forward until he was in contact with his mate from knee to chest. Her shocked gasp made him smile and he gazed at her expressive face as she resembled a startled deer caught in the headlights of an oncoming eighteen-wheeler.

Rhea keenly felt every inch of Tristan that was pressed so tightly against her body and her pulse raced as her skin tingled from the contact. Half of her prayed that he would kiss her and the other half prayed that she was dreaming and would wake up any minute. Rhea found his dominance unbelievably arousing and she was extremely aware of her lack of experience when it came to relationships. She was suddenly afraid that she would seem like a naive adolescent in the face of Tristan's overpowering sexuality and whimpered in panic before looking up into his piercing emerald green eyes.

Uh oh, Rhea though belatedly as she became ensnared in his powerful gaze. Tristan knew that Rhea was overthinking everything and decided to drag her attention back to the present. He looked deeply into her surprised hazel eyes before lowering his head ever so slowly. Rhea held her breath as Tristan's face came nearer and nearer to hers and let out a small gasp as he slowly licked along her trembling lower lip. She felt a surge of heat at the intimacy and grabbed his t-shirt to steady her trembling limbs.

Tristan had to fight everything within him not to just grab her and take her somewhere private to ravish her senseless. That brief taste of her had his head spinning and he shut his eyes while touching his forehead to hers in an attempt to cool his blood. Rhea whimpered again. This time at the loss of contact, and lifted her mouth to find his before her inhibitions took over. Tristan groaned as Rhea's lips met his softly and tentatively and the battle for self-control was lost. He pulled her against his body more tightly and took control of the kiss, pressing his mouth firmly against hers and teasing her with little swipes of his tongue against the seam of her lips. Rhea gasped as Tristan gently bit into her lower lip and he took advantage by claiming her mouth fully and forcefully with his talented tongue.

Rhea felt as if the world was spinning as Tristan asserted his dominance in the most pleasurable of ways. She was amazed at how easy it was to just lose herself in his intoxicating taste. He reminded her of the decadent flavor of dark chocolate and she could gladly stay like this with him forever. Tristan felt his wolf howl in joy and pride as their mate submitted to him willingly. He traced her teeth with his tongue before drawing hers out almost playfully. Tristan suddenly broke the kiss and pressed his forehead against hers once more.

"You sorely test my self-control, my sweet, but we are about to be interrupted and I don't think this particular interruption will be very tactful about the situation. But trust me, we will be continuing this later," he promised.

Rhea's fuzzy brain took a few seconds to comprehend what Tristan was saying and then she blushed a deep red before burying her face in his t-shirt and groaning aloud.

Rhea groaned again and pushed futilely at Tristan's chest to try to get him to move. He didn't budge and she would have been cussing him out if it weren't for the fact that his kiss had left her reeling and she was totally off kilter. She couldn't believe that she had been so brazen.

"In a hurry, Rhea?" Tristan asked lazily.

"No, I told you, I'm hungry. Now move," she demanded, finally finding her voice and her self-respect.

Tristan chuckled but stepped back and grabbed her hand to lead her into the cafe, extremely pleased at her response to their first kiss and elated that she had practically initiated it. He opened the door for Rhea and then led her to a booth in the corner nearest to the door. The cafe was quite busy but the noise quieted down as a number of people averted their eyes when Tristan walked past.

"Oh Lord!" Rhea suddenly said softly, standing up and grabbing her purse. "You're an Alpha aren't you? Jesus!! I am so outta here!!"

Tristan looked at her in shock before gripping her wrist to stop her from running away.

"Rhea, please sit down. I will explain anything you want to know but don't ever run from me, Little One."

Rhea registered Tristan's very serious expression and decided self-preservation would be better served by her sitting down and doing whatever he told her to, until the opportunity to get away presented itself.

"Yes, I am the Alpha of the Forest Pack. How did you guess?"

"You're the owner of Forest Industries, you get to order Aidan around, people stop talking and look down when you walk past them and you just command respect. It's not exactly how betas and omegas behave. Look Tristan, whatever it is you want from me, just tell me now so you can save yourself the effort of pretending to court me or whatever and just get on with business," she said flatly.

"What on earth are you talking about, woman? I'm not pretending to do anything. And how in Luna's name do you know so much about us?" Tristan asked in frustration. His mate was making no sense and he hated feeling so uncertain.

"Tristan, just tell me what you want. Don't play games. I can handle the truth. And I just know these things, okay? Now please just—"

Rhea's speech was cut short by Tristan. "Dammit Rhea, I want you! You are my mate. We were destined to be together. Do you understand the concept of life-mates when it comes to wolves?"

Rhea suddenly stiffened as her gaze fell past Tristan to the doorway of the cafe and she stared in growing horror as panic engulfed her like a tidal wave.

"Oh, hell no, I am not going through this again. Whatever sick game you're playing Mr. Forest, count me out. I've had enough drama with bloody werewolves to last me a lifetime."

Tristan became aware of the bitter scent of her fear and panic. This time he knew it was not directed at him and his wolf growled at the idea that something was causing such terror in their mate. He looked up and his wolf surged fiercely at the image of the man in the doorway of the cafe. He growled under his breath and stood up immediately, barely registering the members of his pack who did the same and moved into defensive positions around his booth.

"Tristan!" the stranger boomed. "It's good to see you again, brother. "

Tristan stood so still that Rhea thought he resembled a stone statue. She would have been more puzzled by his reaction if she weren't freaking out over the fact that her worst nightmare had just walked into the cafe and addressed Tristan as "brother." She should have known that she could never escape his horrific clutches. It was too much to hope that she would be able to live a normal productive supernatural-free life.

"What, no warm embrace? I'm hurt brother," the stranger laughed.

"What do you want Logan? You aren't welcome in this territory and you are no brother of mine," Tristan said coldly.

"Ooh, that one hurt. Can't a guy just stop by to check how his little brother is doing?"

"No. Now leave before I'm forced to remove you."

Logan's cold-black eyes flitted to Rhea and a slow smirk spread across his face.

"Just hand over the hot brunette you have over there Tristan and I'll be on my way. It's not nice to keep a man's property from him," Logan said jovially.

Tristan saw red with those words and had to reign in every instinct he possessed to not rip off Logan's head where he stood.

"It would serve you well to never so much as glance in her direction again Logan. I won't be as lenient with you as I was the last time," Tristan bit out.

Logan's eyes hardened at the reminder of what had transpired between them the last time they saw each other.

"I would have thought you'd avoid interfering with mates Tristan. You know the sacred law. And Rhea over there is most definitely my mate," Logan said cheerfully.

Tristan heard Rhea whimper almost inaudibly and his deadly claws slid out slowly, a clear warning to his brother. There was no way in hell he would be letting him take Rhea. She was HIS mate. Nobody else would be touching her.

"I believe you are sorely mistaken Logan. Rhea belongs to no other wolf but me. You should know better than to quote sacred law to me. Now leave," Tristan said, surprised by how calm he sounded.

"In that case I challenge you to the right to mate with her, brother dearest," Logan growled, clearly displeased with Tristan's claim on Rhea.

"I gladly accept. Now get your scruffy horde the hell off my land before my betas are forced to teach your pack a lesson about the meaning of territory," Tristan growled.

"We will meet again soon Tristan," Logan promised.

Chapter 4

Tristan watched his brother's pack file out of the cafe and he fought the urge to roar at their traitorous impudence. Tristan was the Alpha by right and by strength and he itched to get the fight with his brother done right then and there. Suddenly aware once more of the scent of fear surrounding his mate. Tristan turned sharply, just in time to see Rhea sliding quietly out of the booth.

"Oh no you don't," Tristan bit out, lifting her up and placing her over his shoulder. "I want answers, mate, and I want them now."

Tristan's overwhelming instinct at that moment was to take Rhea somewhere private and claim her in the primitive way of the wolves but his Alpha responsibilities dictated that he finds out exactly why his brother believed Rhea was his mate and why he had dared to resurface in Tristan's territory after all these years. Tristan was pissed beyond belief but he reigned in his wolf and walked out to his car.

"Put me down Tristan, please. I promise I won't say a thing. I'll leave the area and be gone for good. Please, I'm begging you, just let me go."

Tristan registered the note of hysteria in her voice and put her down gently as he reached his car, despite the rage simmering in him. Ignoring the look of relief on Rhea's face, he opened the passenger side door and waited for her to get in.

Rhea thought for a brief second that he was letting her go but then she saw the steely look in his eyes as he waited for her to get into the car and felt her hopes get crushed with that one look. She got in quietly and shuffled as close to the door as possible after he walked to the driver's side. She didn't dare try to run at that moment because she knew he would catch her before she even got out of the car. Rhea registered Tristan's clenched fists and rigid jaw before he got into the driver's seat. She shut her eyes and prayed fervently that this was just a bad dream and that she was sleeping safely in her home. She refused to acknowledge the fact that Logan had just marched back into her life, that he was Tristan's brother and that they were apparently going to fight over the right to claim her. Rhea felt herself being dragged into memories she swore to forget a long time ago and shivered unconsciously as she kept her eyes shut, trying her hardest to think of how she could escape from Tristan.

Rhea's train of thought was interrupted by the feeling of the car coming to a stop. She blinked her eyes open and watched warily as Tristan opened the passenger side door for her.

"Come on Little one. You're safe here. This is my home."

Rhea scoffed at his promise that she was safe but exited the car quietly and walked up the steps leading to the front door. The cabin was huge and she could tell that although it looked rustic, there was plenty of high tech security surrounding the house.

Tristan opened the front door and watched Rhea carefully for her reaction to her future home. Despite his anger and the drama of the last half an hour, he was still anxious about her seeing their home for the first time.

Rhea kept her expression carefully blank as she surveyed her surroundings. The house was clean and neat but still very homely. She could easily envisage sitting in front of the fireplace wrapped tightly in Tristan's strong arms, watching their children play a few feet away.

Whoa woman! Get a grip. Your life is in danger. Again. Don't be fooled by a bloody werewolf, Rhea mentally chastised herself.

Tristan hated the fact that Rhea could so easily hide her feelings from him. He couldn't tell if she was pleased by his home or not but he knew that there were more pressing matters at hand.

"Rhea," he began, "I'm not going to hurt you sweetheart. I need to know why Logan thinks you are his mate."

Rhea cringed at the mention of that monster's name but she analyzed the events that occurred in the cafe and came to the conclusion that either Tristan and Logan truly despised each other, or they were both amazing actors. Her throat ached at the idea that Tristan was as evil as his brother but she decided that she would not volunteer any information until she knew for sure what Tristan's motives were. Her paranoia had served her well in the past and even though her instinct told her that Tristan could be trusted, logic prevailed and forced her to say nothing.

Tristan could see the wheels turning in Rhea's head. After a few minutes of silence he realized she planned on ignoring his question. He ran his hands through his hair in frustration and thought about how he could persuade her to talk. His wolf was extremely agitated that his brother had interacted with his mate before Tristan had found her and her terror at seeing Logan had Tristan's imagination running through the worst possible scenarios. He felt his eyes shift into the inky black of his wolf and his claws cut through the air slowly. Tristan had to fight every urge in his body as his wolf wrestled him for dominance. He felt cold fury as he recalled Rhea's expression at seeing Logan. Beads of sweat gathered on Tristan's forehead as he fought his beast for control.

Rhea watched in fascination as Tristan's eyes changed color, the piercing black making him look dark and deadly. She was shaken out of her funk when his claws slid out and she realized that he was fighting his beast. For some reason, Rhea wasn't afraid of this side of Tristan. She knew to be careful but every instinct in her was urging her to try and calm him down. Rhea approached him slowly and lifted her hand up to his jaw. Her skin tingled at the contact and her breath hitched but she was determined to bring him back.

"Tristan... Come back to me," she urged quietly.

Tristan was losing himself. He could feel the wolf gaining dominance and pushed harder to regain control. Distantly he realized Rhea had approached him and at her timid touch on his jaw he felt the wolf recede abruptly. He shook his head as if to clear it and realized the wolf had lost its rabid fury as soon as he realized they were possibly endangering their mate.

"Oh Luna! Rhea, forgive me Little One. I can't stand the thought of you being hurt and my wolf wants to find Logan and shred him to pieces. I'm so sorry I lost control like that," Tristan said, unable to meet her eyes.

Rhea cupped his jaw more fully and lifted his head so that his eyes met hers. She could see the self-loathing in his eyes but also the anger boiling beneath the surface. Rhea couldn't tell if Tristan was just acting or not but she realized that she truly believed he was being sincere. His reactions were just too primal and spontaneous to be deceptive.

"It's okay. I'm okay. Look, I still don't know whether this is the wisest move but I'll tell you whatever you need to know. For whatever bizarre reason, I trust you Tristan," Rhea said softly.

Tristan felt immense relief as Rhea spoke and then felt his wolf howl happily at her indication that she trusted them. His eyes flared and he stared at her intensely without uttering a word.

Rhea felt more self-conscious the longer Tristan stared at her. The forceful penetrating expression in his gaze made her feel hot and cold all at once and she pulled her hands away from his face abruptly, letting out a nervous breath as she did so. She couldn't believe how bold she was around him and how he so easily made her forget herself. Just five minutes ago she had doubted everything about him and wanted to run as far away as possible and now she wanted nothing more than to have him touch her and never let go. She would consider herself bipolar if she stopped to really think about her behavior.

Tristan saw the uncertainty in his mate's eyes as she pulled away from him and caught her wrist before she could move further away.

"Oh no you don't," he breathed out. "You don't get to just say that and then walk away Rhea."

Tristan used his grip on her wrist to drag her against his body and captured her mouth forcefully before she could protest. He groaned as he once again experienced her sweet taste and felt Rhea place her hands against his chest as he gently but determinedly coaxed her mouth open. All at once the kiss changed from forceful to frenzied. Tristan felt her respond to his aggression and he couldn't hold back anymore. He had his stunning mate in his arms and he could scent her arousal, turning him mindless with need.

Tristan grabbed the back of Rhea's thighs and hoisted her up so that she was pressed firmly against his aching cock. She whimpered at the sensation of him pressing against her core and shifted her hips to feel more friction even as his tongue wickedly dominated her mouth. Tristan growled and tightened his grip on her thighs as he carried her to his bedroom. He broke the kiss to place her on the centre of his bed and paused to relish the view of his mate lying in his domain where she belonged.

Tristan's nostrils flared as he inhaled Rhea's scent and he kicked off his shoes before climbing onto the bed to join his mate. She gazed at him with a sleepy sexy expression and whimpered as Tristan's body covered hers, effectively pinning her to the mattress. Tristan took her mouth again, this time slow and gentle. Rhea responded to his kiss by growing even wetter and she grabbed onto his shoulders to steady herself. She had never felt this all-consuming need before and if she had the ability to think clearly her mind would have been screaming at her to stop before things got out of hand.

Tristan ran his right-hand down Rhea's body as he kissed her, from her back down to her left thigh and held her firmly as he devoured her mouth. He felt Rhea move her hands down his chest timidly and growled as she reached the edge of his jeans. He removed his hand from her thigh and grabbed her hand that was against his lower abs, placing it firmly on his skin under his t-shirt and groaning at the feel of her skin on his. Rhea inched her hands slowly upward, feeling his warm skin under her palms and his firm abdominal muscles. She scraped her nails lightly against his skin and felt as well as heard him growl his approval.

Suddenly Rhea became aware of Tristan's hand lifting her t-shirt and she froze, memories she had buried coming to the surface in a great catastrophic rush. She whimpered again, this time in fear and pulled her hands away from him as if she had been scorched.

Tristan registered the sudden change in his mate and pulled away from her slowly, his heart breaking at the fearful expression in her eyes. He spoke softly to her, trying to get her to come back to the present.

"Rhea, Little One, its okay. You're safe. It's me, Tristan. Nobody is going to hurt you sweetheart," he cajoled gently.

Rhea heard Tristan's calm tender tone and was pulled back to where she was. She buried her face in his neck and sobbed as she recalled the images that had flown through her mind. She knew that she was safe with Tristan and felt so ashamed at her reaction, knowing that it would have hurt him badly as well.

Tristan was once again fuming as he realized that Rhea was terrified of intimacy. His wolf was nearly rabid with fury once again but his instinct to soothe and comfort his mate conquered his urge to rip apart the person who had caused her fear. He chastised himself for moving too fast and pushing her when she wasn't ready.

"I'm so sorry Tristan," she said, pulling backwards and startling him out of his chain of thought. "It wasn't you. I'm just so sorry."

Tristan kissed her cheek gently and brought her back into his arms.

"No my sweet, I'm sorry. I shouldn't have pushed you so fast," he breathed out.

"You are my mate. I will protect you for eternity, " Tristan promised.

"You know you're the only one I'm going to make love to," Rhea was got calm as Tristan reassured her.

Rhea's tiny cold hands pawed at Tristan's muscular broad. Rhea's skin was so sweet, so warm against his mouth. He needed more. He put his hands under her blouse, exploring her warm stomach and the faint outline of her ribs with his fingers.

Rhea moaned at his touch and impatiently pushed him away to shed her shirt, baring her lace encased breasts for him. He moaned in blissful agony seeing her show herself to him. He'd always loved Rhea, but he'd never realized how much it would turn him on and drive him insane to see her creamy mounds framed so delectably. His mouth traced her collarbone to her breastbone to rest between those soft mounds, delighting in the feel of her satiny skin against the sensitive flesh of his lips. He cupped one of her full breasts lovingly even as his mouth descended upon the other sucking at the taut nipple through the lacy fabric.

Rhea writhed and gasped beneath him whimpering in ecstasy even as her head thrashed back and forth on the sand. She was as beautiful as he'd imagined. Her whiskey-colored hair framing her face, her pale skin flushed with passion. He turned his attention to her other breast, pulling the lace away to bare her pink nipple that stood erect, waiting for him to suckle into his mouth. He latched onto it, hungrily suckling the tiny nub into his mouth, even as he reached behind her and unclasped the lacy bra. Now that he'd tasted her flesh, the beautiful lingerie only frustrated him.

Desperately Rhea began to undresshim, and he helped her, the same desire roaring through him to feel her warm, naked body against his skin. When their soft flesh finally met, an electric shock roared through his body. At long last he had someone. Rhea was so soft, so warm.

Full of passion and feral need, Tristan consumed Rhea's mouth again, mating his tongue with hers, groaning as her fingers traced the contours of his muscles and caressed his back. Those delicate hands seemed to be everywhere on his flesh, sending shivers of pleasure down his spine making his pulsing cock throb in agony. He groaned and pushed his pelvis into hers, the friction of their bodies teasing them both.

"Tristan," she gasped. She cried out as his mouth latched back onto one of her pink nipples and suckled, twisted and lathed it with hunger.

"Yes," he growled even as he continued to consume her flesh.

"Don't stop," Rhea ordered forcefully even as she raked his back with her nails.

"Never," he groaned as his mouth trailed downwards kissing the protrusion of her ribs and then making their way to her belly button.

His fingers nimbly undid her jeans and quickly pulled them from her hips, growling in desire at the thong that graced her mound. His mouth kissed the insides of her thighs and all around that small triangle of lace, making her jump as though his lips were shocking her with some kind of erotic electricity. He hungrily inhaled her musk even as he visually assessed her dampness, purring in satisfaction that he'd been the one to cause such passion. He latched his mouth to the fabric, tasting her arousal, smiling as she shrieked and twitched the moment his mouth made contact with her heat.

"Tristan," Rhea wailed in need. " Tristan..." she groaned.

Rhea's pleading cries shattered any control Tristan had left. He ripped the panties from her body and nearly lost it when he stared her glistening sex; shaved and hairless, red and weeping for his attention. He parted her folds and feasted on her, moaning into her softness at the sweet taste of her arousal.

Rhea screeched incoherently at his touch, whimpering with need, but he toyed with her, flicking her clit only for a moment before kissing or licking the juices that coated her.

Just before she cried out in frustration he'd suckle or nip her again, sending her beautiful head thrashing on the sand. Even as he licked and supped upon her sensitive flesh, he pushed a finger deep within her. He wanted to let Rhea know that she was his woman. She was Tristan's and Tristan's alone. He was going to take his time with her.

The heat was almost unbearable; her soft walls gripped his cock longingly. He inserted another finger and moved them within her slowly and gently at first, and then with more force and fervor. Her pelvis moved in tandem with his thrusts, her body coated his fingers with its juices, her hands balled up with need.

"Please," Rhea demanded, her voice hoarse from desperation. "Please Tristan."

Tristan looked up at her flushed body, her almost green eyes, her tousled hair and smiled at her. Taking pity on her, he latched his mouth over her clit suckling hard until she came screeching and bucking beneath him.

For a moment, he closed his eyes and took a deep breath struggling for control. It would be wrong to claim her. She didn't know his "dark secret." Still Tristan could hear the pounding of her heart, the blood throbbing in her sex, in the artery in her groin...

It took all of Tristan's control as he groaned in agony, forcing himself away from her weeping folds and back up her body delighting in the salty taste of her sweat, the musky scent in the air of her arousal.

Rhea reached out to run her fingers through his hair, those tiny fingers on his skin delighting his senses making his moans of need echo her own keening cries. His mouth supped its way up her neck, and back to her mouth, kissing her deeply, letting her taste herself on his lips. Suddenly she became more aggressive. With deft fingers, she unbuttoned his pants and put her hands inside to feel him.

Her soft hand wrapped around his cock stroking him, spreading the moisture of his arousal around the throbbing head with her thumb. It drove him insane to have her touching him while his body was imprisoned in his clothing.

Tristan's wolf growled impatiently and wanted only Rhea. He removed his pants and his boxers noting her wide-eyed stare with satisfaction. There was something about seeing her angelic eyes staring in amazement that nearly broke him and when she reached out once again and wrapped her slender fingers around him. He gasped in agony. It had been so long since he'd had a woman. Too long. For a moment all he could do was stare at that delicate hand wrapped around his throbbing erection and watch in mesmerized rapture as she stroked him. He groaned at her touch and closed his eyes for a moment as an image of her beautiful mouth devouring his cock flashed before his mind.

Not this time, he told himself.

Fearing to lose the last threads of control he took her tiny hand in his and held it still.

"Do you want this, Rhea?" he growled. Hoping against hope.

She didn't answer. Instead, she reached out with her other hand and pulled him down upon her again, kissing him passionately and forcing her tongue into his mouth.

He smiled at her unspoken demand. Even in bed she was stubborn and willful.

He kissed her with the same intensity, slipping his fingers back into her folds, stroking her sex, rubbing her clit, making her even hungrier for another release. In moments she was writhing beneath him again with need, both hands clinging to his shoulders as he assaulted her with his tongue and his questing fingers. When she was mindless with need, he took his impressive length in his hand and pushed it against her opening, slowly, trying to be mindful that her last penetration had been brutal. Whatever pain she'd last experienced he wanted to erase with pleasure.

They both groaned as he inched inside her. Tristan knew he was big for her. Still, Rhea was unbelievably tight around him, and he filled her so fully that they both lay still panting with the sensation. Tristan kissed her ear and then her lips. He worked his way down to her breast, suckling on her aching nipple. Rhea groaned and he felt her squirm beneath him. Then he started thrusting with agonizingly slow, steady strokes, watching himself disappear within her depths in rapt concentration.

She moaned beneath him and clasped his shoulders with her tiny hands, holding on as her body spun out of control with sensation.

"Tristan," Rhea moaned breathlessly. The pleading sound of his name on her lips sent a shiver down his spine.

He thrust harder even as he found every sensitive spot on her body with his fingers, making her writhe and squirm beneath him, smiling at his ability to fuel her passions so easily. She was beautiful in the throes of lovemaking and he wanted to watch her face as she came yet again at his expert touch. She whimpered and tossed her head from side to side, her fingers raked his back causing him to shudder deliciously, and in return he lightly twisted one of her hardened nipples making her squeak in bliss.

He slipped his hand between their bodies, flicking her clit as he thrust, earning a delicious whine from her lips and he watched in delight as he worked her into the frenzy of another orgasm. She came with a keening cry, her body convulsing beneath him, her sex gripping his cock. For a moment he almost lost control. However, in all his long years, Tristan had mastered the art of lovemaking. He wasn't ready to find his release yet. He had so much more pleasure to offer her with his body and his power.

She relaxed and nuzzled against him after she came down from her second orgasm, but he chuckled in her ear. "Oh no, my little love" he whispered in a dark, dangerous, masculine voice. "Our evening is far from over."

Rhea's eyes looked up at him uncomprehendingly. She could only coo in contentment as her response. Tristan growled possessively. This beautiful, delicate creature in his arms was HIS!

He began to kiss her hungrily then, his earlier tenderness turning to forceful passion. She obliged him, mating her tongue with his, suckling on it, nipping at his lips even as he nipped at hers. His hand palmed her breast and his hips began to thrust against hers again.

She groaned into his mouth as her body responded to his passion.

"You are mine, Little One," he growled in the language of the woods. "I am going to fuck you until your only thought is my body in yours. I'm going to make you scream my name in ecstasy."

Rhea didn't know what his words meant but whimpered at the sound of his dark, dominating voice. Her delicate fingers turned to claws as they raked down his back hungrily.

"That's it my little kitten," he continued. "I'm going to ignite the flames of your body like no man has ever done for you before. You're mine. MINE!"

Tristan felt his wolf start to morph. but he clenched his fist in her hair and with every last shred of his control he forced his beast down. Now was not the time for his dark secret. He wanted to pleasure Rhea. He didn't want to cause her alarm. Tristan focused on plundered her mouth once again, mating his tongue with hers fiercely and ground his hips against hers, stimulating her aching clit.

"And soon, little love," he growled, panting into her ear once again, "I'll claim your heart. I'll devour you and mark you as mine; my true mate. You are mine and no one else's.

She was gasping and moaning beneath him as he pounded her now. He took her legs in his arms and draped them over his shoulders groaning as he penetrated her dripping sex even deeper.

"Tristan" she cried as she built, her tiny claws drawing blood as they sunk deep into his muscular arms.

"You are MINE!" he growled into her ear.

This time her moan was a scream and her body convulsed beneath him, her tight walls gripping spasmodically around his cock. He came with the roar of his wolf, as he rode out their mutual orgasm.

Finally, as his breathing settled and her whimpers subsided, he caressed her hair from her face. Her eyes were closed, but he connected with her mind and felt her body still tingling with little shock-waves from her orgasm.

Soon enough Tristan's cock was hard again. He put it up against Rhea's pussy. He rubbed it around her lips making her moan his name in pleasure multiple times. He slipped his cock in only a few inches fucking her slowly before he moved a little faster going into her deeper. Soon enough Tristan was ready to cum in Rhea's tight pussy his cock pulsing and his balls getting those tingly sensations. Soon enough he was ready and he came into his mate, kissing her hard on the mouth.

"Are you all right?" Tristan whispered. Tristan was worried that he was too rough for her.

"Mmm," she replied in dreamy contentment and Rhea smiled up at her love.

"You are amazing, Rhea," he breathed, kissing her lips tenderly. "So incredible, I can't believe I've actually found you. You are not leaving my site anytime soon." he whispered. Tristan was delighted that Rhea was his.

For now, under the stars, Tristan was happy as his Rhea nuzzled against him in the warm afterglow. Rhea couldn't believe she felt so completely comfortable. Rhea wrapped her arms around Tristan. She closed her eyes and thought back to their love-making earlier. It was the best sex of her life- wild, erotic, passionate, and... she'd never had so many orgasms before. It had been a blissful day. Magical. What had happened between Tristan and her was beyond Rhea's wildest imagination.

Tristan nodded, not believing what he had longed for was coming true. He had a true mate. He had a true mate. He HAD a true mate. He drew Rhea into a deeper embrace and kissed her. He knew Rhea was his now.

THE END

www.ingramcontent.com/pod-product-compliance
Ingram Content Group UK Ltd.
Pitfield, Milton Keynes, MK11 3LW, UK
UKHW041643190726
13854UKWH00006B/2666